WINTER

To Colin and Peedie P.

Also by Mairi Hedderwick

Katie Morag and the Big Boy Cousins
Katie Morag and the Tiresome Ted
Katie Morag and the Two Grandmothers
Katie Morag Delivers the Mail

First U.S. edition
Library of Congress Catalog Card Number 88-81822
ISBN 0-316-35406-6
10 9 8 7 6 5 4 3 2 1
Printed in Hong Kong

P.D. Peebles' Summer or Winter Book

Mairi Hedderwick

Little, Brown and Company
Boston   Toronto   London

P.D. Peebles likes waking everyone up, SUMMER

P.D. Peebles does NOT like getting dressed, WINTER

or WINTER.

Breakfast is P.D. Peebles' favorite time, SUMMER

or SUMMER.

Sometimes, P.D. Peebles does NAUGHTY things, WINTER

or WINTER.

Other times, P.D. Peebles does grown-up things, SUMMER

or SUMMER.

At bedtime, P.D. Peebles plays hide-and-go-seek, WINTER

or WINTER.

Until he remembers it is story time, WONDERFUL time, SUMMER

or SUMMER.

Afterward, almost every time, P.D. Peebles falls fast asleep, WINTER

or WINTER.

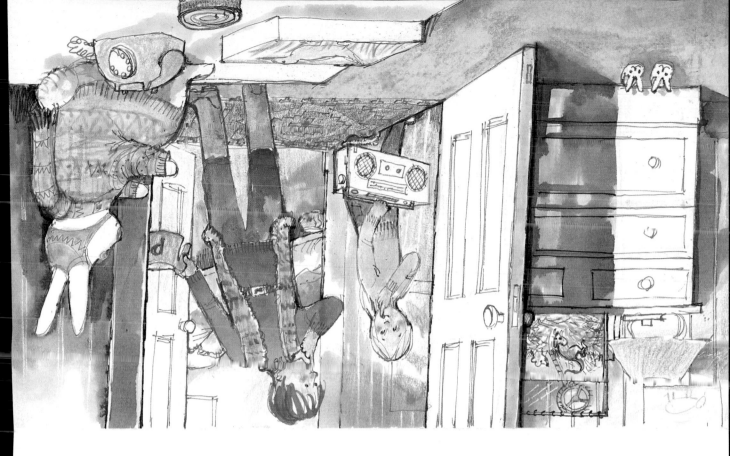

WINTER

or SUMMER.